I DISCOVERED HOW MUCH I LOVED ART THE
summer I spent with my grandmother and father
in Michigan. Grandma was an artist; she drew and
painted so beautifully! Grandma even told me that
I was a natural artist, so I couldn't wait to take Art
at school next fall when I got home to California.
I only had one problem left—tests. I just couldn't
seem to pass them.

In loving memory of Violet Chew, who

taught me the art of seeing.

Patricia Lee Gauch, Editor

G. P. PUTNAM'S SONS
A division of Penguin Young Readers Group.
Published by The Penguin Group.
Penguin Group (USA) Inc., 375 Hudson Street, New York, NY 10014, U.S.A.
Penguin Group (Canada), 90 Eglinton Avenue East, Suite 700, Toronto, Ontario M4P 2Y3, Canada
(a division of Pearson Penguin Canada Inc.).
Penguin Books Ltd, 80 Strand, London WC2R 0RL, England.
Penguin Ireland, 25 St. Stephen's Green, Dublin 2, Ireland (a division of Penguin Books Ltd).
Penguin Group (Australia), 250 Camberwell Road, Camberwell, Victoria 3124, Australia
(a division of Pearson Australia Group Pty Ltd).
Penguin Books India Pvt Ltd, 11 Community Centre, Panchsheel Park, New Delhi - 110 017, India.
Penguin Group (NZ), 67 Apollo Drive, Rosedale, Auckland 0632, New Zealand (a division of Pearson New Zealand Ltd).
Penguin Books (South Africa) (Pty) Ltd, 24 Sturdee Avenue, Rosebank, Johannesburg 2196, South Africa.
Penguin Books Ltd, Registered Offices: 80 Strand, London WC2R 0RL, England.

Published simultaneously in Canada.
Manufactured in China by South China Printing Co. Ltd.

Design by Semadar Megged.   Text set in 14-point AT Garth Graphic.
The illustrations are rendered in pencils and markers.
Library of Congress Cataloging-in-Publication Data is available upon request.

ISBN 978-0-399-25703-2
1   3   5   7   9   10   8   6   4   2

The Art of Miss Chew

PATRICIA POLACCO

G. P. Putnam's Sons • An Imprint of Penguin Group (USA) Inc.

I was back in California, and I loved school. Hard to believe, because once I had a lot of trouble reading, but not anymore. And I really liked my new teacher, Mr. Donovan. He was from Ireland and had sky-blue eyes, a laugh that sounded like bells ringing, and a great Irish accent. He loved telling stories about his family back home, especially about his father.

Seemed like he always had a smile on his face.

But he didn't have a smile the day he handed back my first social studies test. I could feel my face get real hot when I unfolded it. An F. Again.

The trouble was everyone read faster than me. Even though I knew the subject real well, I'd run out of time before I was finished. I started having stomachaches when I knew a weekly test was coming up.

Mr. Donovan finally sat me down. "You know the subject, Trisha. What you need is extra time." He started giving me the time I needed and, sure enough, I began passing tests.

But that didn't help my other problem. There was no real art class in my new school, just art on a cart for thirty minutes once a week.

Then one day Mr. Donovan saw one of my drawings. He picked it up and hung it on the bulletin board. "Patricia, you have remarkable talent!"

All of the kids in class crowded up to look at the picture.

"Man, oh, man, can you draw," Davey Mulford remarked.

"Wow!" Rick Schubb agreed.

Even Neonne Price, who never spoke to me because she was so popular, was impressed.

I felt so proud.

It wasn't a day later when Mr. Donovan told me about Miss Chew, head of the high school art department. "She has a special program for young artists on Tuesdays and Thursdays. When I showed her your drawing, she said she wanted you in her special class. Now, what would you be thinkin' of that, Miss Trish?"

I loved drawing. Sometimes when I was drawing, I'd forget to breathe! I danced on air all the way home that day. I couldn't wait to tell my mother.

That first Tuesday, I'd never walked so fast in my life as I did to get to Miss Chew's class on time. I had never seen a room like hers: windows that went from ceiling to floor, giant easels at one end, rows of drying racks at the other, and paint everywhere.

I didn't know anybody!

Then Miss Chew breezed into the room. Her smock was so covered in paint it was a painting in itself. She was tall and slender, and she spoke with a Chinese accent. "We have a new student today," she said, motioning toward me with her beautiful long fingers. "Her name is Ther-esa Barber!"

Theresa? *No,* I wanted to shout, *my name is Patricia!* But Miss Chew had already spun around and was passing out sketchbooks. From that day on, I was Ther-esa.

I could barely understand Miss Chew's accent. "In this class we are going to learn to speak another language." She touched her heart. "The language of art." *Art, a language?* But Miss Chew went on. "It isn't spoken, it is the language of emotion and images.

"But first," she told us, "you need to learn to see! *Seeeeee!*" She plopped down two saltshakers in the middle of the table. "Open your sketchbooks, take up your pencils. Now, draw the shakers, but first, young friends, *see them.* Don't just look at them, see them!"

"See how the light dances through the glass and makes a shadow pattern on the table?" Yes, I saw it! "Draw it," said Miss Chew.

"See how you can make your pencil line darker, and lighter?" She changed the line from dark to light. Yes, I saw that, too.

"Yes, Theresa," Miss Chew said. "You have it.

"Now do your drawings again. Move the shakers. Off center. Let them run off the page. On purpose. Make them bigger, get the dancing light as it makes its shadow," she sang as she moved from table to table.

She made us draw those shakers six times in six different ways!
At the end of the day, she said, "Take your sketchbooks
everywhere with you! First see . . . then draw."

I couldn't wait. I took my sketchbook everywhere with me. On the bus home, I drew people sitting in their seats. Even the bus driver. When I got home, I drew apples in a bowl, and my cat, Tillie. After dinner, I made my mom and my brother, Richie, sit so I could draw them.

"Ain't you got no homework?" my brother groaned.

"This is homework," I said. "Sit a little longer. I almost have you."

The next day, after I had finished my assignment, I asked Mr. Donovan if I could make a drawing of his "da"— his father—from the photo on his desk. I tried to remember everything Miss Chew told me.

The next art class, Miss Chew called me up to her desk. Everyone else had handed in one or two sketches. I had done over twenty.

"Your drawings are very good!" Her eyes smiled as if we had a secret. "The cat, the apples, your mother and brother . . . you've captured every detail. I particularly like your use of negative space."

Negative space?

"See this drawing, Theresa? What do you see?" She held up a picture.

"Two people looking at each other." Anyone could see that.

"Now, Theresa, instead of looking at the two faces, look at what is between them."

Nothing. Wait . . . "A . . . a . . . tall, stemmed cup."

"First you read negative space! Now you are reading the actual object."

What an idea! I started looking at all of my own pictures for negative space.

I was so happy. But a few weeks later, Mr. Donovan was called
to the office. When he came back, his eyes were red. He couldn't
seem to talk. He just stared out of the window. Finally he spoke.

"Me da died today," he whispered. Our whole class got out of
our seats and tried to comfort him.

He left for Ireland the next day. That is when we got Mrs.
Spaulding, a substitute. She never smiled.

Worst of all, when I was taking my weekly test, she came up
behind me and ripped the paper out from under my pencil.

"Time's up," she barked.

"But Mrs. Spaulding, I'm not finished. Mr. Donovan always lets me have extra time because—"

"I'm not Mr. Donovan, and when I say you are finished, you are finished."

Of course, I failed the test. That's when she got just plain mean.

"Your time would be better spent studying for your tests instead of leaving this school to take art classes!" she hissed. "And I'm going to see if I can make that happen."

I tried to be brave and not tell Miss Chew, but in class I began to cry and blurted out the threat that Mrs. Spaulding had made.

Miss Chew began to shake her head slowly. "Theresa," she said. "You say you can't read fast enough to finish your tests?" I nodded. "I watch you draw, and you begin a drawing by drawing what is in negative space!"

I remembered the picture of the two girls facing the glass.

"When you see a word, I think you don't see letters at all at first. I think you first see the space around them. The pattern they make."

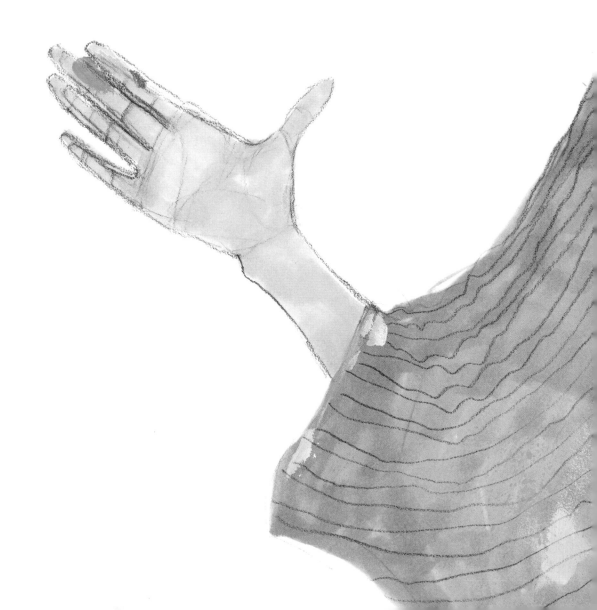

"No wonder your reading takes you so much time!" Miss Chew said.

I smiled, but I still wasn't quite sure what she meant.

"I know someone I think can help. A reading specialist. No one is taking you from this class."

I sprang to my feet and hugged her.

"And tomorrow, Theresa, I am assigning you an easel. You are not only ready for painting, maybe you can be part of the high school Spring Art Show."

The following day, Mrs. Spaulding announced we would take a timed citywide test that would determine what classes we would take next year. We'd have forty-five minutes to finish.

I only finished half the test. I knew my art class was over.

But when I told Miss Chew, she said, "We'll just see about that." With my mom's permission, she would take me herself to see her friend, the reading specialist.

After class, Miss Chew took me to her car. A convertible! As we drove off, the car sounded like it was growling, and I loved it when we drove by my school and Mrs. Spaulding actually saw us.

Dr. McClare played what seemed like a hundred reading games with me, but I wasn't afraid. I knew he was trying to help.

When he finally called Miss Chew in, he said, "You are spot-on, Miss Chew. She reads patterns, not words. This takes time."

Miss Chew wanted a meeting of "all the players." Everyone came: the principal, Mrs. Spaulding, Miss Chew, Dr. McClare, and my mother.

Mrs. Spaulding said the extra art class was "simply a distraction. Trisha is drawing instead of studying."

Miss Chew said, "But she needs extra time to finish tests—all tests."

When she and Dr. McClare said that I see things differently than most students, Mrs. Spaulding scoffed, as if to say *What could an art teacher know about how a child learns. I don't tell you how to teach a child to draw!* It was as if she didn't think art teachers were real teachers, that maybe art wasn't even a real class.

Mr. Donovan came back exactly two days later. I couldn't help myself. I ran to him and hugged him. "I am so glad you are back," I said. When someone else told him what Mrs. Spaulding was trying to do, he got really red in the face.

And I don't know exactly what happened after that day, but it seemed that Mrs. Spaulding was no longer needed as a substitute. Not in the whole school! So I went on to Miss Chew's class every Tuesday and Thursday.

Of course, as soon as Mr. Donovan gave me extra time when I took my tests, I passed them with flying colors.

I decided to use the sketch of Mr. Donovan's father for my first painting. When Miss Chew saw it, she just stood there and looked at it. "Theresa, this sketch is so full of emotion and love—you have most certainly learned the language of art. Mr. Donovan will be so moved."

When I finished the painting, she said, "Theresa, this painting is *going* to be part of the art show. You will be the only exhibiting artist who isn't a high school student."

I couldn't believe it—me . . . ME, in the Spring Art Show!

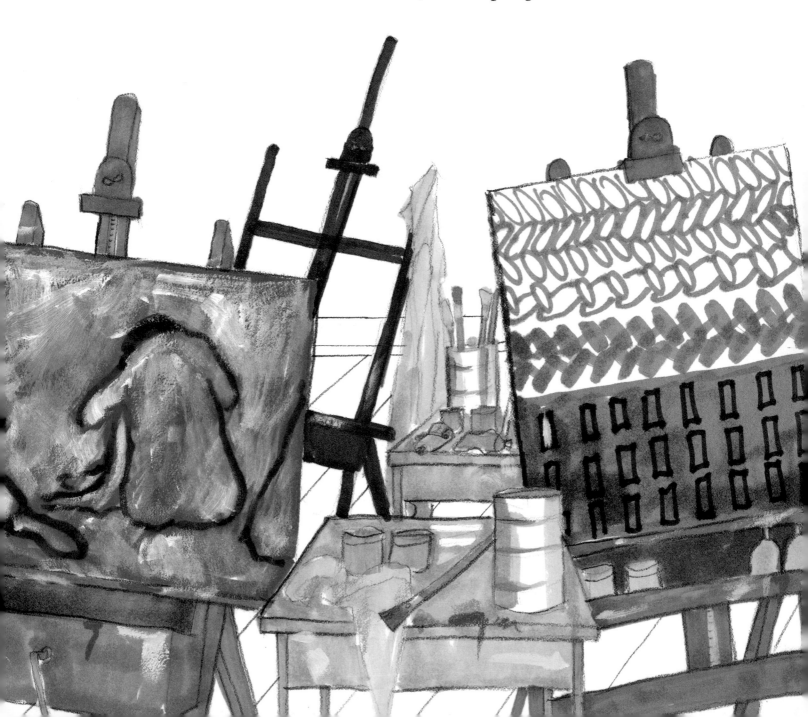

Later that day, Miss Chew asked me to stay after class. She handed me a package wrapped in bright red tissue paper and said softly, "We Chinese believe that red brings luck. And Ther-esa, remember this ancient Chinese proverb: Yesterday is history. Tomorrow, a mystery. Today . . . a gift—that is why it is called 'the present.'" She smiled.

When I opened the gift, I caught my breath. It was one of Miss Chew's painting smocks! For me. I wanted to cry. When I looked in her eyes, she had tears, too.

Only a week later, I wore my new smock to the art show.

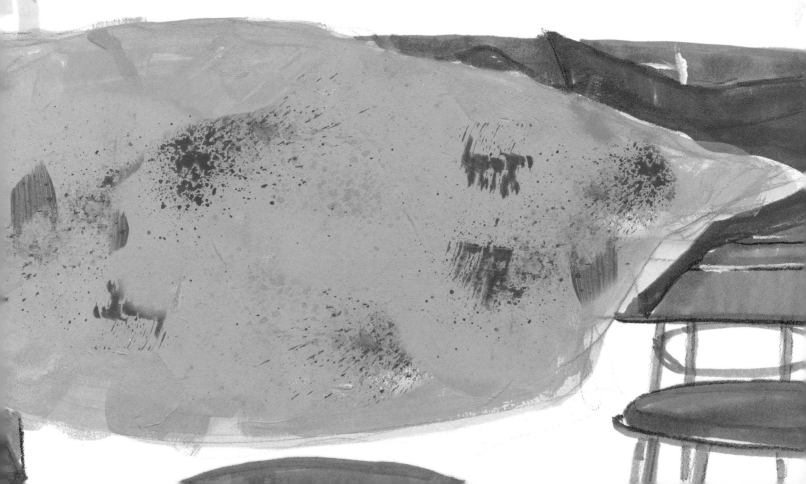

Light was dancing off the mirror chandeliers. Our paintings were everywhere. I was so proud. Then I saw Mr. Donovan standing in front of my painting of his father. He couldn't speak. He took my hand and squeezed it. Miss Chew came up to us. She looked so radiant. "It's beautiful, isn't it," she whispered to him.

I looked at the two of them. Miss Chew was right. This moment was a present. It turned out to be the defining moment in my young life. I was set on a course to be an artist—it could be no other way. Thanks to the art of the amazing Miss Chew.